To my wonderful buddy Mark. Hooray!
– Eric

To Zoe, Dylan and Ben x
– G.L.

First Edition
Kane Miller, A Division of EDC Publishing
Text copyright © Eric Ode 2020
Illustrations copyright © Gareth Llewhellin 2020

All rights reserved.
For information contact:
Kane Miller, A Division of EDC Publishing
PO Box 470663
Tulsa, OK 74147-0663
www.kanemiller.com
www.usbornebooksandmore.com

Library of Congress Control Number: 2020930619

Manufactured by Regent Publishing Services, Hong Kong, China
Printed August 2020 in Dongguan, Guangdong, China

ISBN: 978-1-68464-114-7

2 3 4 5 6 7 8 9 10

Hooray, it's GARBAGE Day!

Eric Ode • Gareth Llewhellin

Kane Miller
A DIVISION OF EDC PUBLISHING

Something's coming down the street,
rolling with a rumbling beat.

A clashing, crashing, noisy treat.
Hooray, it's GARBAGE DAY!

Something's moving big and slow.
Something's growling loud and low.

Can you guess? I bet you know.
Hooray, it's GARBAGE DAY!

GROWL

GRRRR

PURRRR

What a wild and rocking sight.
Yellow lights are flashing bright.

Will it stop? I think it might.
Hooray, it's GARBAGE DAY!

One garbage truck that roars about.
Two workers give a friendly shout.

Three garbage cans sit side by side.
Four bedroom windows open wide.

Five children wave and give a cheer
to say that GARBAGE DAY is here!

What a big and noisy ride!
Give them room, now. Step aside.

Watch that claw; it opens wide!
Hooray, it's GARBAGE DAY!

It gives a hiss. It gives a sigh.
It grabs a can and lifts it high.

It dumps it in, and, my, oh my!
Hooray, it's GARBAGE DAY!

Find a box. A wagon, too.
We can be a garbage crew.

Here we go! There's work to do!
Hooray, it's GARBAGE DAY!

One orange juice carton.
Toss it in.

Two cans for the recycle bin.
Three bottles. They'll recycle too.

Four chairs to paint and make like new.
Five toys to fix and give away.

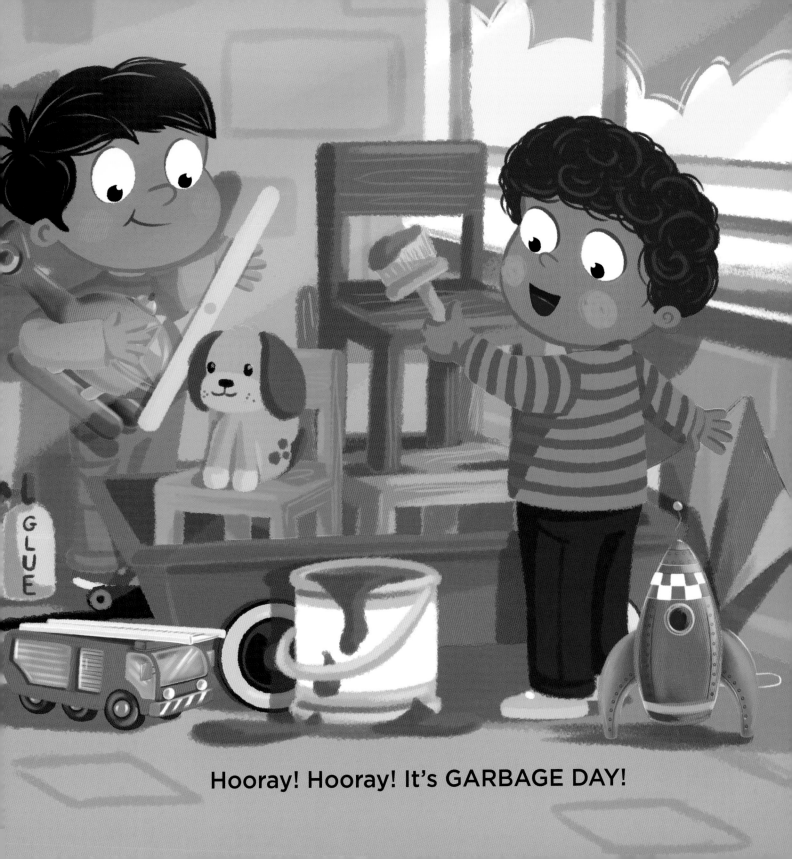

Hooray! Hooray! It's GARBAGE DAY!

The compost pile can make its meals
of coffee grounds and apple peels.

How good a clean-up morning feels!

Hooray, it's GARBAGE DAY!

HONK!

Now that truck is on its way.
So much to do. No time to stay!

It gives a honk as if to say,
Hooray, it's GARBAGE DAY!

One garbage truck is moving on.
Two workers wave,
and then they're gone.

Three garbage cans sit side by side.
Four puppies take a wagon ride.

Five children know they'll wait, and then
GARBAGE DAY will come again!